CODES & CIPHERS

Mark Fowler

Designed and illustrated by
Radhi Parekh

Edited by
Sarah Dixon

Contents

Series Editor: Gaby Waters
Assistant Editor: Michelle Bates
Puzzle checkers: Rachael Robinson and Richard Dungworth

Before You Start

Secret messages, coded diaries, cryptic inscriptions and mysterious symbols . . . all these and more lie in wait on the pages ahead. Some of the puzzles are moderately tricky, while others could prove fiendishly difficult. Look carefully at the documents and illustrations which accompany each puzzle. They contain all the information you require to find the solution. If you need help, turn to pages 42-43 for clues to point you in the right direction. If you are totally stumped, you will find all the answers on pages 44-48.

You can pick out a puzzle to solve at random – if you dare. But if you tackle them in order, you will be able to follow the story of five intrepid adventurers as they grapple with a series of exciting challenges.

WANTED

Five adventurers. Reply with credentials to Box No. 15

The adventure begins when a strange notice appears in the Global Herald. Out of thousands of replies, five individuals are selected to take part in an intriguing mission. They each receive instructions summoning them to Almaro City in the States of Enigma. Clutching packed suitcases and proof of their identity, they report to room 501 of the Rialto Hotel. Here, a mysterious figure in dark glasses checks their credentials . . .

ASSOCIATION OF NEWS JOURNALISTS

OFFICIAL PRESS CARD

NAME: BEN HARVEY
INVESTIGATIVE REPORTER

NEWSPAPER:
THE DAILY PLANET

AXO - 94

PASSPORT

FEDERATION OF THE STATES
OF ENIGMA

Name of bearer: Sally Cameron
passport no.: 894621 D
Occupation: Explorer

Farmassi
Institute

Name: Carrie Jones PPD
STATUS: Junior research
scientist
DEPARTMENT: Aeronautics

MACAVITY'S
ACADEMY
OF
DETECTION AND
FORENSIC INVESTIGATION

MEMBERSHIP CARD

NAME: KATE JONSON

TOP SECRET

24 - I.I.N - 9

INTERNATIONAL
INTELLIGENCE NETWORK

NAME: MAT SMITH
SECURITY CLEARANCE: ALPHA X2
OPERATIONAL ID: PORTIA 006

The mystery figure hands each person a sealed brown envelope then walks slowly out of the room, leaving a file on a table as he goes. The file contains two small cuttings and a letter . . .

To Mat Smith, Kate Jonson, Ben Harvey, Sally Cameron and Carrie Jones

Let me introduce myself. I am Thomas Hudson, a retired adventurer. After years of painstaking research, I have discovered the location of a hoard of lost treasures from the ancient civilization of the Bilongi Islands. Sadly, my treasure-hunting days are long over, so I am giving you the chance to find the Bilongi treasures.

It will not be an easy task. First, each of you must take on a challenging and possibly dangerous mission:

Mat Smith: you must discover the name of the building where the Red Panther Spy Ring set up its secret headquarters over forty years ago.

Kate Jonson: you must find out where Ben Pierce's gang of Wild West outlaws hid the loot from the Maryville train robbery.

Ben Harvey: you must uncover the true identity of the seventeenth century adventurer known only as Le Capitaine.

Sally Cameron: you must find the name of the mountain where the ancient Bilongi warrior, Hapu, built his stronghold.

Carrie Jones: you must retrieve a coded message from the mountain refuge of the famous mystic, Lo Chi. The message is hidden in Lo Chi's secret chamber.

Each of you has been given a sealed envelope. These contain instructions to lead you to the starting point of your investigations. Do not open your envelope until you have left the hotel and do not reveal its contents to anyone.

You have exactly four weeks to complete your missions. Then you must return to this room at 6pm to take up my ultimate challenge.

Be warned: all five of you must succeed in your tasks. If just one of you fails, you will never discover the secret of the treasures' hiding place.

Good luck,

Thomas Hudson.

WHO'S WHO OF ADVENTURERS
HUDSON, THOMAS: adventurer; born December 9th 1926, Longville; joined International Intelligence Network, 1949; led operation against Red Panther Spy Ring, 1953; set up cattle ranch near San Fernando, 1955; moved to Chateau des Tours, 1960; led expedition to far east, 1974; crash landed on uninhabited island in Bilongi Group, September 1974; located secret refuge of 14th century mystic, Lo Chi, 1975; retired to hermitage in Aldheim Mountains, 1989. PUBLICATIONS: *Le Capitaine: The Man Behind the Myth.* LEISURE INTERESTS: Cryptography; astronomy.

Two thousand years ago, the Bilongi civilization came to an abrupt end when the islands were struck by a series of extremely violent earthquakes. The islanders sailed away in search of new lands. This ancient painting is said to show the Bilongi islanders hiding hundreds of gold and silver treasures before they set sail. These treasures have never been found.

Coded Telegrams

As he hurries away from the Rialto Hotel, secret agent Mat Smith tears open the envelope containing his instructions. Inside, he finds the following message: "LEFT LUGGAGE OFFICE, CENTRAL AIRPORT, ESCOVIA: LOCKER 13". Quickly, Mat hails a taxi and soon he is on his way to the airport. He boards the next plane to the distant republic of Escovia, ready to begin his search for the secret headquarters of the Red Panther Spy Ring.

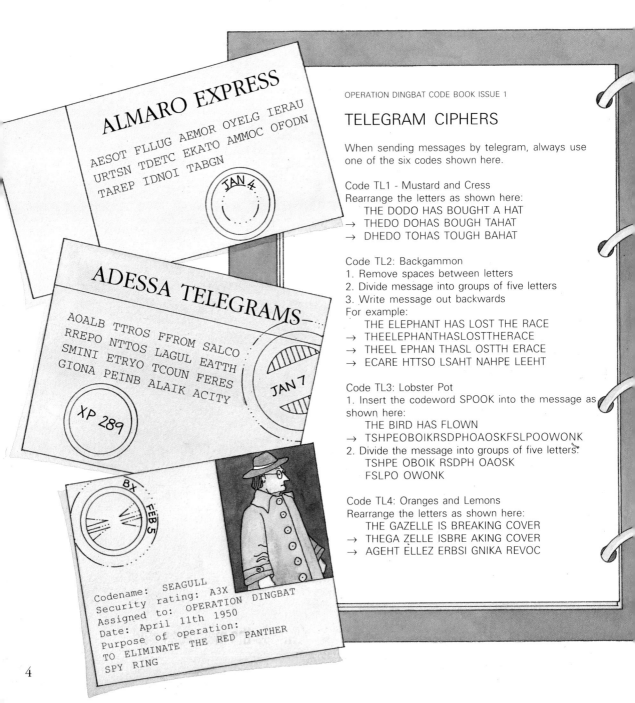

ALMARO EXPRESS

AESOT FLLUG AEMOR OYELG IERAU
URTSN TDETC EKATO AMMOC OFODN
TAREP IDNOI TABGN

JAN 4

ADESSA TELEGRAMS

AOALB TTROS FFROM SALCO
RREPO NTTOS LAGUL EATTH
SMINI ETRYO TCOUN FERES
GIONA PEINB ALAIK ACITY

XP 289

JAN 7

Codename: SEAGULL
Security rating: A3X
Assigned to: OPERATION DINGBAT
Date: April 11th 1950
Purpose of operation:
TO ELIMINATE THE RED PANTHER
SPY RING

BX FEB 5

OPERATION DINGBAT CODE BOOK ISSUE 1

TELEGRAM CIPHERS

When sending messages by telegram, always use one of the six codes shown here.

Code TL1 - Mustard and Cress
Rearrange the letters as shown here:
    THE DODO HAS BOUGHT A HAT
→ THEDO DOHAS BOUGH TAHAT
→ DHEDO TOHAS TOUGH BAHAT

Code TL2: Backgammon
1. Remove spaces between letters
2. Divide message into groups of five letters
3. Write message out backwards
For example:
    THE ELEPHANT HAS LOST THE RACE
→ THEELEPHANTHASLOSTTHERACE
→ THEEL EPHAN THASL OSTTH ERACE
→ ECARE HTTSO LSAHT NAHPE LEEHT

Code TL3: Lobster Pot
1. Insert the codeword SPOOK into the message as shown here:
    THE BIRD HAS FLOWN
→ TSHPEOBOIKRSDPHOAOSKFSLPOOWONK
2. Divide the message into groups of five letters:
    TSHPE OBOIK RSDPH OAOSK
    FSLPO OWONK

Code TL4: Oranges and Lemons
Rearrange the letters as shown here:
    THE GAZELLE IS BREAKING COVER
→ THEGA ZELLE ISBRE AKING COVER
→ AGEHT ELLEZ ERBSI GNIKA REVOC

Nine hours later, Mat's plane touches down in Escovia. He makes straight for the left luggage office and retrieves a package from locker 13. It contains a bugging device, an old identity card, a blue file, and five telegrams covered with blocks of meaningless letters. Mat realizes that these are coded messages. Flipping through the file he finds a section headed "Telegram Ciphers". With the help of these pages, he can make sense of the telegrams.

Code TL5: Deadly Nightshade
Encode the message as shown here:
THE JACKDAW HAS CONTACTED THE RAVEN
→ T E A K A   H S O T C E T   E A E
  H J C D   W A C N A T D H R V N
→ TEAKA HJCDW HSOTC ACNAT ETEAE DHRVN

Code TL6: Laughing Demons
Rearrange the letters as shown here:
THE LEOPARD IS WORKING FOR
THE ENEMY
→ THELE OPARD ISWOR KINGF
  ORTHE ENEMY
→ THALE OPERD ISNOR KIWGF
  OREHE ENTMY

QST

TSOPS OEOAK GSUPL
OLOFK RSOPM OMOAK
CSAPW OROEK DSPPA
ONOTK HSEPR OAOGK
ESNPT,OSOHK ASVPE
OIONK FSIPL OTORK
ASTPE ODOTK HSEPA
OLOBK OSNPI OROEK
SSEPA OROCK HSIPN
OSOTK ISTPU OTOEK

FEB 17
AX 397

SENDERO TELEGRAMS

TEGEN OALAD RVNRM AEFOS
EGLCR AULAR YUSRE OTUVI
LACOE LNEPR AINTL TOAAB
OIEER NRSAC HNTTT ISIUE
IETFR DNIYE DATEI PNHRN
FLRTR ITAOS

MAR 11

HALVANIA TELEGRAMS

TOLEA	GUSLF	ROOFA	LCMNW	EHEVE
IDANT	IFDED	ANIAR	RELTE	DASBO
NITNF	ILIRA	TORSB	UTRED	PAITH
ERNSP	LANNI	NGNEW	OPORA	TIENA
TUNKN	OWNLO	CAOIO	NPTSS	IBEYO
THLRR	ESEAR	CHEST	ABEIS	HMLNT

APR 4

What do the messages say?

Ben Pierce's Book Cipher

To Danny Heape and Jake Sharp –
We're counting you in on our next
job. In two days time, Joe Gough
will hand you a piece of paper with
your instructions. You must use the
numbers on the piece of paper to
find certain words in the book that I
have enclosed with this letter.
Together, the words form a
message. The numbers will look
something like this:
25.7.6 26.3.8 25.1.5
The first number is a page number.
The second is a line number. The
third is a word number.

Memorize this letter, then
destroy it.

Pierce

GOLD FEVER - CHAPTER 15

BANDITS!

At that moment, Will Gable spotted five horsemen on the hills behind us. "Bandits!" he cried. We leaped back onto the wagon as Will set the horses into a gallop. At once the five horsemen gave chase, racing down the hill toward us.

"Faster!" I cried. "They're gaining on us." We had to reach the safety of the next settlement. We raced along the rough track, sending up a choking column of dust. The noise of the wheels and the horses' hooves was deafening.

Faster and faster we went, the passengers clinging on for dear life as the driver whipped the horses into a frenzy. But the bandits were still gaining on us. The track steepened and to our right it dropped sheer to the valley floor below. The horsemen were now almost upon us. I could see their masked faces and their pistols glinting in the sunlight.

At that moment, we rounded a turn in the track, and there was the small town of Maryville. I heard one of the outlaws cry "Stop!". Then, firing their pistols into the air, they turned and fled.

46

Clutching her envelope, trainee detective Kate Jonson embarks on her search for the place where Ben Pierce and his gang hid the loot from the Maryville train robbery. Kate's instructions contain just five words: "JAKESVILLE: JOE HANK'S GENERAL STORES". After a long train journey, Kate arrives in the small town of Jakesville. At the General Stores, the owner hands her a parcel containing an old book of Wild West memoirs, a letter and a scrap of paper covered with rows of numbers. Reading the letter, Kate quickly realizes that the scrap of paper holds the key to a secret message hidden in the book.

47.9.6 47.13.4 46.1.4

47.12.12 46.7.12 47.20.1

47.1.6 47.3.8 47.7.2

47.3.12 47.11.6 47.19.2

47.17.10 46.3.10 47.4.1

47.12.1 46.10.7 47.3.12

47.5.8 47.7.2 47.18.7

47.9.9 47.5.10 47.18.4

47.6.1 47.6.10 47.11.2

46.7.8 46.11.2 46.12.8

46.16.12

We made our way from Maryville to Frontier Town without further incident. Here we exchanged our wagon and horses for sturdy mules and left most of our possessions at the mail office. From now on, we had to travel across uncharted territory. There were no tracks, only mile after mile of rugged wilderness. We trudged to the upper reaches of the Klondike River. But as we climbed to Dead Man's Pass, fate unleashed a train of terrible events. Suddenly we heard an ominous rumbling sound.

"It's a landslide" cried Little Joe. "Run for it!"

We raced for shelter as the rocks came crashing toward us with incredible force. Then suddenly Annie May slipped on the narrow path. As she fell down the steep mountainside, she managed to grab hold of an overhanging rock. Josiah Gough struggled to reach her. The landslide was almost on top of us. Just as huge boulders crashed onto the path, Annie and Josiah dived for safety.

Miraculously everyone survived. But when all was calm, we realized that we had lost three quarters of our supplies. You can hardly imagine the hardships of the next weeks. When at last we reached Oliver Town on June 31st, we were almost delirious with exhaustion. We staggered into the town more dead than alive.

47

NOTICE

THE MARYVILLE STEAM COMPANY PROUDLY ANNOUNCES THE COMPLETION OF THE LONG AWAITED RAILROAD FROM FORT BLOOMSBURG TO MARYVILLE. OVERCOMING NUMEROUS NATURAL OBSTACLES AND WORKING TIRELESSLY IN HOSTILE AND REMOTE TERRAIN, WE HAVE BUILT A LINE THAT SURPASSES ANY IN THE GREAT WEST. THE OFFICIAL OPENING ON JULY 13TH WILL BE ATTENDED BY GOVERNOR JAMES CHICHESTER III AND THE RAILROAD CHIEF, SAM HAYLEY. THE LINE WILL BE OPEN TO PASSENGERS FROM JULY 19TH.

Maryville Mail Train

First class

One adult

May 31st 1884

5

What is the message?

The Playing Card Cipher

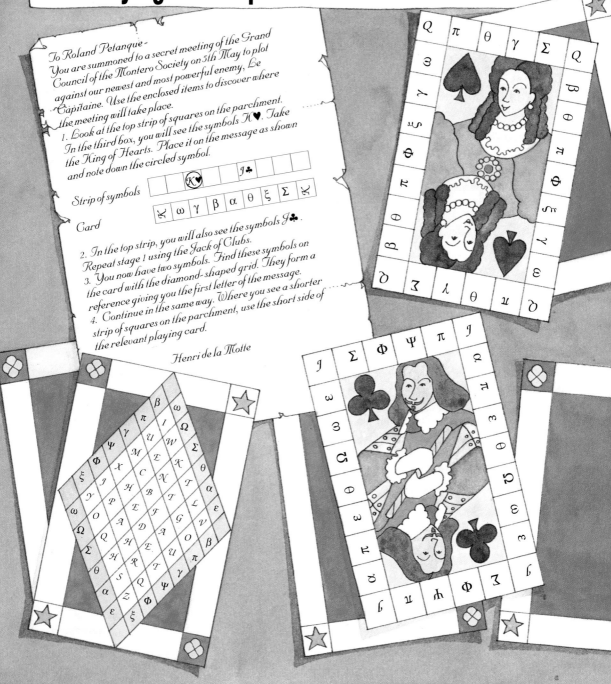

To Roland Petanque –
You are summoned to a secret meeting of the Grand Council of the Montero Society on 5th May to plot against our newest and most powerful enemy, Le Capitaine. Use the enclosed items to discover where the meeting will take place.

1. Look at the top strip of squares on the parchment. In the third box, you will see the symbols ℋ ♥. Take the King of Hearts. Place it on the message as shown and note down the circled symbol.

Strip of symbols

Card

2. In the top strip, you will also see the symbols ℐ ♣. Repeat stage 1 using the Jack of Clubs.
3. You now have two symbols. Find these symbols on the card with the diamond-shaped grid. They form a reference giving you the first letter of the message.
4. Continue in the same way. Where you see a shorter strip of squares on the parchment, use the short side of the relevant playing card.

Henri de la Motte

Ace reporter Ben Harvey sets out to discover the real name of the mysterious seventeenth century adventurer known only as Le Capitaine. Ben's envelope contains the following instructions: "OLD MUSEUM, PLACE DE BRIOCHE, VALERS: CASE 81ZX". At the museum, Ben finds display case 81ZX. Next to a tattered sheet of parchment and some strange playing cards, he sees an old letter.

The letter reveals that the contents of the case once belonged to a member of a sinister organization called the Montero Society. The members of this society arranged to meet to plot against their sworn enemy, Le Capitaine. Using the parchment and the cards, Ben can discover where the meeting was held.

Where was the meeting?

The Ancient Symbols of Takosu

After nine days on a rusting steamer, intrepid explorer Sally Cameron arrives on Lakala, the only inhabited island in the remote Bilongi Archipelago. She reads through her mission instructions for the hundredth time: "LAKALA ISLAND: THE OLD CUSTOMS HOUSE".

On the waterfront Sally finds the Customs House, long deserted. Inside, she finds a parcel addressed to her. It contains a letter from Thomas Hudson, two pages from a book about ancient Bilongi languages and a parchment covered with strange symbols. From the letter she learns that she must decipher the symbols to begin her search for the place where Hapu built his stronghold over two thousand years ago.

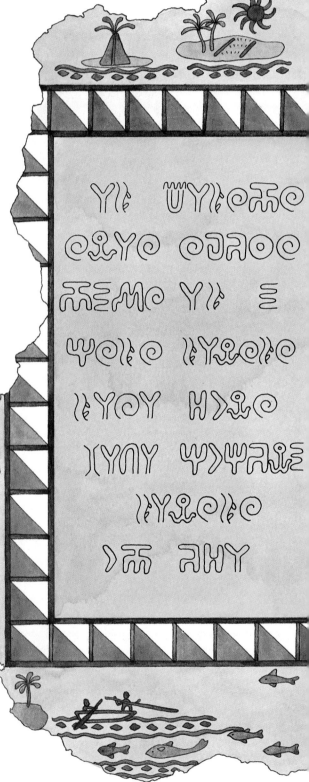

Dear Ms Cameron,

This ancient painting comes from the Bilongi island of Takosu. The symbols in the middle of the painting form a series of sentences in Takosu's ancient language. These reveal the name of the island where Hapu was born. You must translate the symbols then go to the island to continue your quest.

To make sense of the symbols, you must discover which of them corresponds to which English letter. To help you, I enclose two pages from the Official Survey of Ancient Bilongi Languages.

Good luck,

Thomas Hudson.

P.S. When you reach the island where Hapu was born, you must follow the island's only river upstream through thick jungle. After eight miles, you will find a painted stone covered with inscriptions which you must translate.

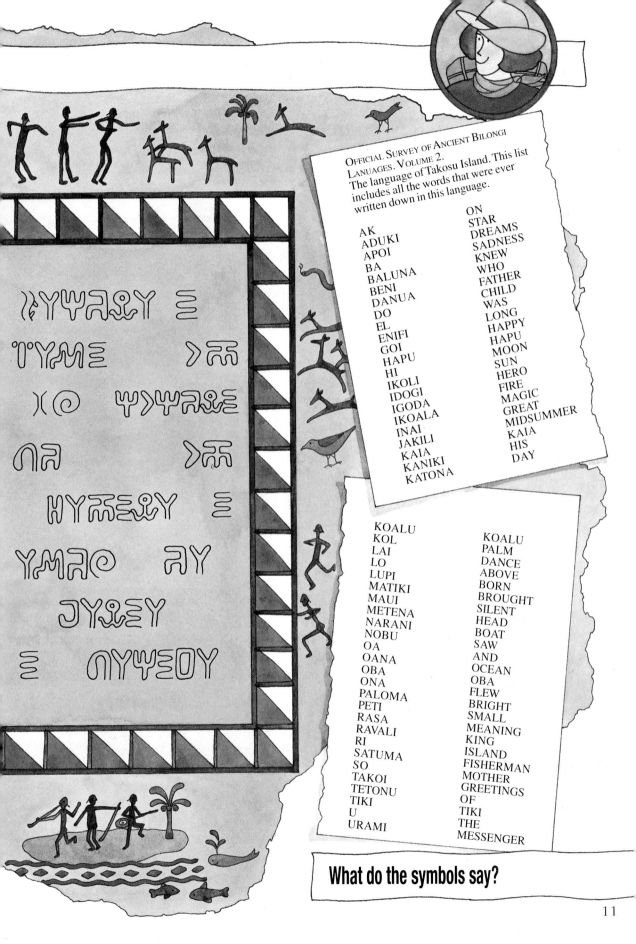

OFFICIAL SURVEY OF ANCIENT BILONGI LANUAGES. VOLUME 2. The language of Takosu Island. This list includes all the words that were ever written down in this language.

AK
ADUKI
APOI
BA
BALUNA
BENI
DANUA
DO
EL
ENIFI
GOI
HAPU
HI
IKOLI
IDOGI
IGODA
IKOALA
INAI
JAKILI
KAIA
KANIKI
KATONA

ON
STAR
DREAMS
SADNESS
KNEW
WHO
FATHER
CHILD
WAS
LONG
HAPPY
HAPU
MOON
SUN
HERO
FIRE
MAGIC
GREAT
MIDSUMMER
KAIA
HIS
DAY

KOALU
KOL
LAI
LO
LUPI
MATIKI
MAUI
METENA
NARANI
NOBU
OA
OANA
OBA
ONA
PALOMA
PETI
RASA
RAVALI
RI
SATUMA
SO
TAKOI
TETONU
TIKI
U
URAMI

KOALU
PALM
DANCE
ABOVE
BORN
BROUGHT
SILENT
HEAD
BOAT
SAW
AND
OCEAN
OBA
FLEW
BRIGHT
SMALL
MEANING
KING
ISLAND
FISHERMAN
MOTHER
GREETINGS
OF
TIKI
THE
MESSENGER

What do the symbols say?

11

Lo Chi's Cryptic Board Game

Tearing open her envelope, junior scientist Carrie Jones finds the following message: "LAPSANG TEA WAREHOUSE, SAITONG: ASK FOR HOO MING". After a long journey, Carrie arrives in the far eastern city of Saitong, the starting point of her search for Lo Chi's secret refuge. She hurries through a maze of backstreets to the Lapsang warehouse and steps inside a vast, deserted storeroom. "Hoo Ming?" she calls nervously.

To my devoted followers,

I have been forced to flee from my home in Saitong, for I am accused of plotting to poison the Prince of Xo Han. I am innocent of this crime, but my enemies are powerful and plan to throw me into the fearful dungeons of Saitong. Therefore I have decided to take refuge in the Chi Nen Mountains. To find me, you must uncover my trail of secret instructions. I have concealed the name of the place where you must go first in the board game. Place all the pieces on the board so that the symbols on the pieces match the symbols on the squares beneath. Take care that no two pieces overlap. At the end, ten squares will be left uncovered. Read the letters on these ten squares, going down the left hand column, then down each of the other columns in turn.

May you grow in wisdom and happiness,

Lo Chi

An old man emerges from the shadows and hands Carrie a wooden box. She opens the box and carefully lifts out an old game board, thirteen game pieces and a yellowed letter. The letter reveals that four hundred years ago, Lo Chi left a trail of cryptic instructions so that his followers could find their way to his secret refuge. The first set of instructions are concealed in the boardgame.

What do the instructions say?

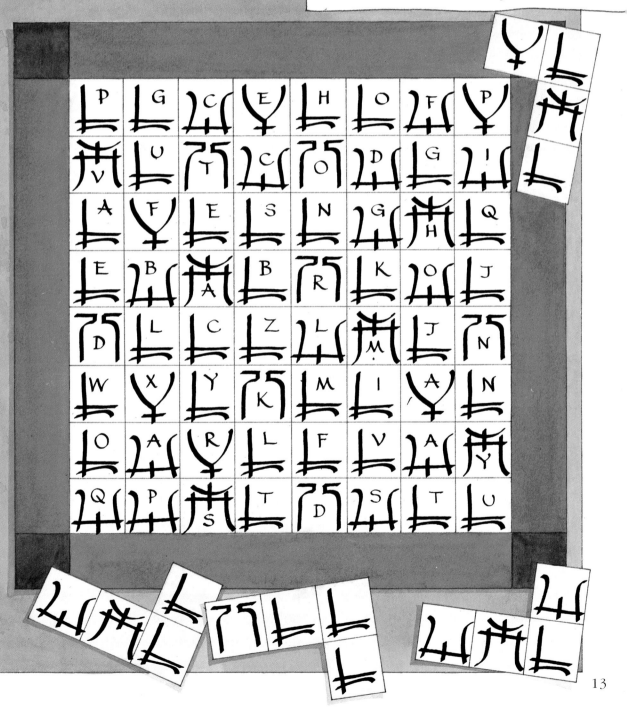

13

Scrambled Symbols

Acting on information in the coded telegrams, Mat Smith goes to the Ministry of Counter Espionage in the North Escovian city of Balaika. Forty years ago, this was the base for a secret operation codenamed Dingbat which aimed to smash the Red Panther Spy Ring. Ministry officials check Mat's identity, then lead him to the Archive Rooms, deep underground. Mat searches among shelves of dusty files and finally unearths a battered folder marked DINGBAT PHASE 2.

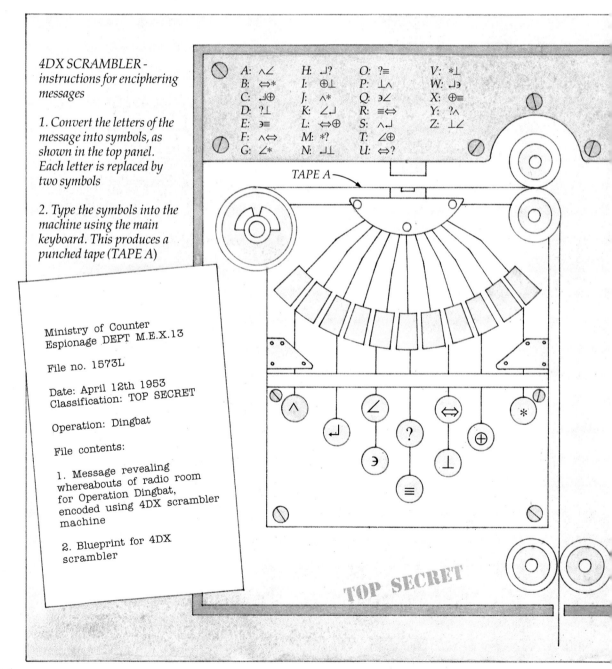

4DX SCRAMBLER - instructions for enciphering messages

1. Convert the letters of the message into symbols, as shown in the top panel. Each letter is replaced by two symbols

2. Type the symbols into the machine using the main keyboard. This produces a punched tape (TAPE A)

Ministry of Counter Espionage DEPT M.E.X.13

File no. 1573L

Date: April 12th 1953
Classification: TOP SECRET

Operation: Dingbat

File contents:

1. Message revealing whereabouts of radio room for Operation Dingbat, encoded using 4DX scrambler machine

2. Blueprint for 4DX scrambler

Inside, he finds two strips of paper punched with symbols and a blueprint for an ingenious scrambler machine. The strips of paper were produced by the scrambler and reveal the location of a secret radio room used for Operation Dingbat. If Mat works through the encoding instructions on the blueprint in reverse order, he can make sense of the symbols.

What do the symbols say?

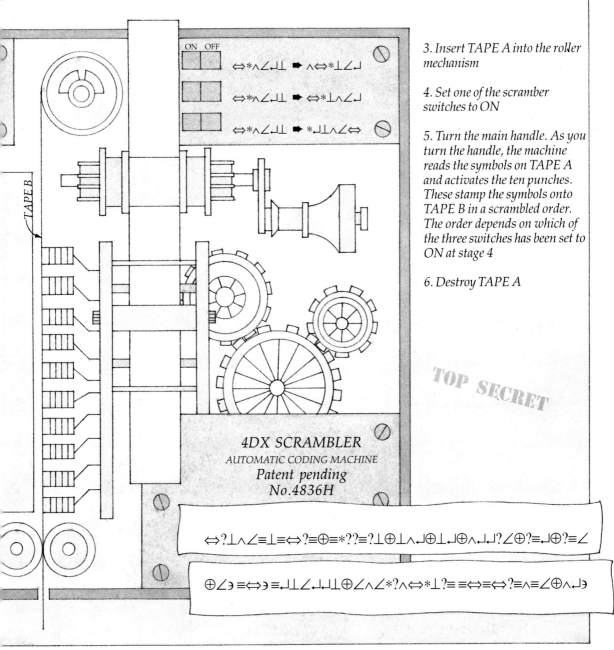

3. Insert TAPE A into the roller mechanism

4. Set one of the scrambler switches to ON

5. Turn the main handle. As you turn the handle, the machine reads the symbols on TAPE A and activates the ten punches. These stamp the symbols onto TAPE B in a scrambled order. The order depends on which of the three switches has been set to ON at stage 4

6. Destroy TAPE A

4DX SCRAMBLER
AUTOMATIC CODING MACHINE
Patent pending
No.4836H

Joe Gough's Coded Diary

From Ben Pierce's coded message, Kate Jonson knows that the attack on the Maryville mail train was led by an outlaw called Joe Gough. At the library in Jakesville, Kate hunts through a collection of old copies of the Western Star newspaper in search of more information. From these, she learns that Gough was arrested in 1885. In his possession was a coded diary which is now kept at the James Chichester Museum in the bustling city of San Fernando.

Kate sets out on the long journey to San Fernando. At the museum, she finds the diary in a display case. It is open at the entry for May 31st 1884, the day of the attack on the train. With the help of a label in the case and a strange coding device, Kate can decipher the entry.

JOE GOUGH – LEGENDARY OUTLAW

Joe Gough was a member of Ben Pierce's band of outlaws, who terrorized the Maryville territories from 1865 until 1885. The gang became notorious when they held up the Maryville mail train in 1884, stealing a large consignment of gold bound for the San Fernando Bank. The gold was finally recovered thirty years ago by local rancher, Tom Hudson.

It is thought that Gough was the brains behind the gang's activities. He started in life as a lawyer, but when he was accused of corruption in 1872, he fled into the Red Mountains where he joined Pierce's gang. His diary provides a fascinating account of the outlaw's life. It is written in an elaborate code. First Gough changed the punctuation then he scrambled the order of the lines in the entry with the help of an unusual coding device.

May 31st '84

♣ Distant engine
signal! We'd attack
would force the driver. To stop at their
minutes ... Later the train came into view
the mail van. And grabbed the sacks
I set off. With Hank Knott at sunrise and
Heape and Jake Sharp! Were aboard and
Davenport. We raced back to our horses
of gold.
"Prepare," to strike. I yelled at Hank:
"Pass waiting for the train!" to appear at
we took up. Our positions in the Klondike.
Halt the plan was working. We rushed -
we both knew. The plan by heart Danny
were led. By our old enemy marshal. Jack
(the train) screeched to a sudden
noon exactly. We heard the sound of a
horsemen riding in our direction. They
but at that moment I saw a column of -
"To the train!" smashed open the doors of
♦ Davenport. Rode straight at him. Hank
tore along the mountain trails, driving.
But Davenport was hot on our heels. We

WANTED
DEAD OR ALIVE

was in the marshal's clutches ...
For the secret hideaway, but when we
loot in a secret. Place then fled into the
horses. And galloped away from the scene
location of our hideaway. We buried the
arrived Pierce. Was waiting for us with
scrambled to his feet, but seconds later he
(staggering under the weight of the gold)
next county.
Last we managed to outride. Our pursuers
the rest of us leaped back. Onto our
he had even. Handed over details of the
our horses as hard as we could. And at
suddenly I saw Hank Knott stumble
to Fort Davenport. And had betrayed us
bad news. Hank Knott had been. Taken
we laid low until nightfall then set out.

OUGH

OUS OUTLAW

Elaborate coding device used by Joe Gough to encipher his diary

Original line number

| 1 | 2 | 3 | 4 | 5 | 6 | 7 | 8 | 9 | 10 | 11 | 12 | 13 | 14 | 15 | 16 | 17 | 18 | 19 | 20 |

| 19 | 18 | 15 | 8 | 6 | 12 | 11 | 17 | 1 | 10 | 4 | 14 | 7 | 3 | 2 | 16 | 13 | 20 | 5 | 9 | 19 | 18 | 15 | 8 | 6 | 12 |

♠ ♥ ♣ ♦ — Coded line number

♠ ♥ ♣ ♦

What does the diary say?

The Montero Meeting

To Henri Mayenne,

You are hereby appointed as official secretary to the worthy Society of Montero. You will keep a record of all Montero Society activities. Meetings of the Grand Council shall be recorded in code using the following method:

- remove all spaces and punctuation from the matter to be encoded

- replace the letters A, E, I, O and U with numbers or symbols. Select three different numbers or symbols to stand for each letter. Each time you encode a letter, use any one of the three relevant numbers or symbols.

By the order of the Duke of Thierry, Grand Master of the Montero Society

6SS13 N&STH !M2! T!NG 1P9N!DTH 2D¶K2*FTH! !RR
Y4NN 3¶NC9DT H4TL!C &P!T4!N 2H6DTH W&R
T!D1§ R4CT !V!T 52SF* R 6 TH! RDT8 M9 F8 V!M!M
B!RS3F TH9S1 C!!TYW !R9C&7GH TR2D H4N D!DD¶
R!NG TH !6TT2 MPT T1 ST!&L TH2 *RL&N D*D
84M3ND S4NDTH2Y& R!N* W R3 TT8 NG8N C 4R C!L
L2 P R!S 1N T H9 D §K! D!M6 ND!D TH6T W!

From the playing card message, Ben Harvey knows that the members of the sinister Montero Society met at Chateau Lot over four hundred years ago to plot against their arch enemy, Le Capitaine. Ben travels to the chateau, hoping to find out more. When he arrives, he explains his mission to the present owner, the Countess of Montmorency.

D5SC*V!R TH! !D !NT!TY*F L! C4P!T& !N!S1T H4TW!
C6N! L8M5 N&T! H5M 1NC!4NDF* RALL 5MM !D!&T
!LYR *L4N D P!T6N Q7! L! &P!D T 1 H!S F !2T 4NN
*§NC!N G TH &T H9H&D H!R9D 6 C!RT4!N M
*NS8!7R TH3M 6 ST*D8S C*V!R H!S TR¶! !D2N T!TY
M*NS!!¶RTH3M6S !S *N! 1FT H!M1ST C ¶N N!NG
R3G§!S !NTH!W H*L! K8 NGD1 M TH! D¶K2 W6
SPL! 4S!D &T T H9 N!WS& ND 3FF!R !D T* R!W 6RD M
*NS52§RT H3M 6SW!THF5 V2 H§NDR! DFR6N CS5FH!
S¶C C !9DS

Monsieur Thomas
Fencing Master
31, Rue de la Pique

In the large library, the countess hands Ben a leather bound book, which falls open at a page covered with strange writing. The countess explains that the page contains coded details of the secret meeting. With the help of a letter that he finds tucked inside the cover, Ben can decipher the writing.

What does the writing say?

The Mystery of the Tiki Inscriptions

Sally Cameron has discovered that the warrior Hapu was born on the island of Tiki. Now she must set sail for this island and follow its only river upstream to find a painted stone.

Armed with charts and helpful notes from the Bilongi Institute of Exploration, Sally reaches Tiki and slowly rows up the river. She abandons her boat at the foot of a waterfall and hacks her way through the thick jungle that lies along the bank. Scratched, bruised and close to exhaustion, she finally reaches the stone. On it is painted a snake decorated with strange inscriptions. With the help of her notes, Sally can translate the inscriptions into English.

What do the inscriptions say?

THE BILONGI INSTITUTE OF EXPLORATION

Dear Sally,

We have no record of inscribed stones on Tiki Island, but any inscriptions would be in the same language that was used on nearby Tahini Island. I enclose a copy of some Tahini Island inscriptions that were found during a recent expedition. Each symbol corresponds to one English word, but the order of words is not the same as in English.

I hope this information will help you in your mission,

Anita Raia

Head of Exploration.

Tahini Island Inscriptions	Translation
	Kinja gave a papaya to Hapu
	The earthquake destroyed the temple
	The evil magician left the islanders
	Oba sang to Kaia
	Adiki struck Oba
	Adiki sailed away
	A firebird came to Tiki
	One firebird gave a seashell to Kinja
	Another firebird went to Guana
	Oba went to the temple
	Kaia ruled the islanders
	One group sang to Hapu
	The fearsome magician led the dance
	Kinja left Guana

The Grids of Go

To my devoted followers,

To find my next set of instructions, you must use the papers that you will find with this letter. They consist of four square grilles, a grid of letters stamped with the seal of my friend the Prince of Go, and a large scroll of symbols.

- Look at the first symbol on the scroll. (You will find the first symbol in the top left hand corner)
- Find the grille with this symbol in the corners
- Lay the grille over the grid of letters
- Take the letter that lies beneath the number 1 on the grille. This is the first letter of the message
- Do the same for the second symbol on the scroll (the second symbol is underneath the first)
- Use the same method to reveal the rest of my message. When you come to a symbol for the second time, lay the grille over the grid of letters as before, but take the letter under the number 2
- When you reach the end of the first column on the scroll, translate the symbols in the second column.

May you grow in wisdom and prosperity,

Lo Chi

O	G	H	T	P	G	O
O	T	E	A	O	D	O
A	M	H	E	I	A	X
F	N	N	I	F	T	N
N	D	D	H	K	E	R
E	E	E	T	F	O	R
P	E	O	B	H	S	E

The message hidden in Lo Chi's cryptic board game directs Carrie Jones to the Grand Palace in the ancient city of Go. After an almost endless journey across the plains of Lo Sung, she arrives at Go's Main Station. She makes straight for the Grand Palace where she finds a collection of objects and papers that once belonged to Lo Chi.

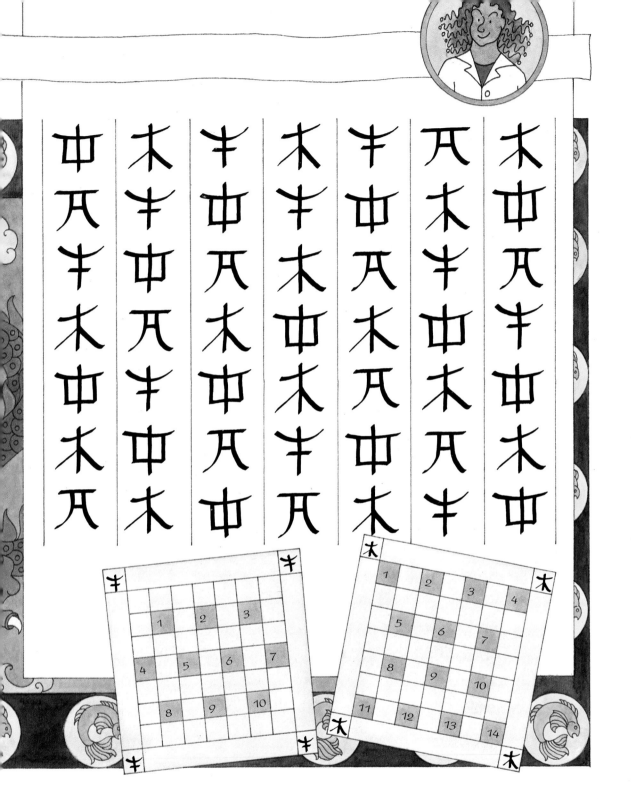

They consist of a scroll with elaborate symbols, a letter, four cards with number grids and a page with a grid of letters. Following instructions in the letter, Carrie can discover where Lo Chi hid the next set of instructions in the trail leading to his secret refuge.

Where are the instructions hidden?

Morse Transmission

May 16th

[dots and dashes handwritten message]

Mat Smith makes his way through the Kamarov Forest to the ruined tower used by Dingbat agents over forty years ago. Inside the tower, he finds a trapdoor. It opens to reveal a flight of steps leading down to a small underground chamber. On an old desk, Mat spots a piece of paper covered with dots and dashes, together with a code book, an old newspaper and a radio transmitter. The dots and dashes form a secret message. With the help of the code book and the newspaper, Mat can figure out exactly what it says.

What does the message say?

OPERATION DINGBAT
CODE BOOK ISSUE 2

CODE 4976: HAIRPIN BENDS

ENCODING INSTRUCTIONS

1. Remove all punctuation and word spaces from the message.
2. Divide the text into GROUPS of eight letters.
3. Select a four letter KEYWORD from the previous day's Global Herald. It must not contain any letters that appear in the first eight letter GROUP of the message.
4. Write down a REFERENCE for the KEYWORD. A typical REFERENCE looks like this: 2 23 4. This means that the KEYWORD is in the second column, line 23 and is the 4th word in the line. When counting the line numbers, do not include the newspaper's title, headlines, headings, or subheadings.
5. Take the first KEYWORD and the first GROUP of letters and scramble them. For instance, if the first GROUP was MEETINGS and the first KEYWORD was LOCK, the jumbled version could be MLEEOTICNGSK.
6. Write down the scrambled KEYWORD and eight letter GROUP after the REFERENCE.

7. Select a second KEYWORD, making sure that it does not include any letters that appear in the second eight letter GROUP of the message, and write down its REFERENCE. Scramble the KEYWORD with the second GROUP of letters, then write them down after the reference.
8. Continue in the same way until the whole message is encoded. Then translate everything into Morse Code, and transmit on frequency GF7.

MORSE CODE

A ·—	N —·	1 ·————
B —···	O ———	2 ··———
C —·—·	P ·——·	3 ···——
D —··	Q ——·—	4 ····—
E ·	R ·—·	5 ·····
F ··—·	S ···	6 —····
G ——·	T —	7 ——···
H ····	U ··—	8 ———··
I ··	V ···—	9 ————·
J ·———	W ·——	0 —————
K —·—	X —··—	
L ·—··	Y —·——	
M ——	Z ——··	

15th May 1953

Issue no. 1756

THE GLOBAL HERALD

RED PANTHER STRIKES BALAIKA CITY

A RELIABLE SOURCE LAST NIGHT DISCLOSED THAT A SINISTER SPY RING IS OPERATING IN BALAIKA CITY Members of an organization calling itself the Red Panther Ring have infiltrated the world famous Pyrites Research Institute. They have stolen top secret formulas which could enable them to hold the entire country to ransom. The spies are said to be extremely well organized and highly dangerous.

Reports suggest that the spy ring may be led by the notorious criminal mastermind, Lev Sapova. Wanted on numerous counts of conspiracy and espionage, Sapova is undoubtedly the most dangerous – and elusive – criminal operating in Escovia today.

UNDERCOVER INVESTIGATION

It is understood that an undercover investigation is being carried out by agents from the International Intelligence Network. However, as each day passes, the dangers increase. The leaders of the Red Panther must be caught before they strike again.

CONTENTS

REGATTA RETURNS

The much loved soprano Carlotta Regatta has announced that she will come out of retirement for a gala performance on July 8th at the Borlotti Opera House.

MYSTERY HEIR SOUGHT

Lawyers are still trying to trace a descendant of the seventeenth century adventurer, Le Capitaine. The mystery descendent has inherited the magnificent Chateau des Tours in the world famous Amouret Valley. He is thought to live somewhere in the States of Enigma, but so far all attempts to trace him have failed.

NEWS IN BRIEF

World famous detective, Archie Malloy has been awarded the Order of Merit for solving the case of the Sarga

Explorers in r Bis that they ha Mammoth ous that the ike an had been usands of years.

Cut Out Letters

In San Fernando, Kate Jonson discovers that a member of Pierce's gang was captured by Marshal Davenport during the attack on the Maryville mail train. He was taken to Davenport's headquarters at Fort Chichester where he betrayed his fellow bandits. Kate travels to the fort, now carefully restored, where some belongings of the captured outlaw are on display. Among them are a letter, two metal disks and a scrap of paper with a sentence made up from cut out printed letters. Behind the innocent words, there is a cunningly concealed message.

What is the hidden message?

The Fencing Master's Papers

Ben Harvey knows that a character called Monsieur Thomas was hired by the Montero Society to discover the real identity of their arch enemy, Le Capitaine. Monsieur Thomas ended his days as fencing master to the Regiment of Muskateers. At the regiment's modern headquarters, Ben unearths objects and papers that once belonged to Monsieur Thomas. They include two game counters, a letter and a picture covered with symbols.

To Monsieur Thomas
You must leave all communications to the Montero Society at a secret message point. The enclosed engraving contains a coded message revealing the location of this place. To decode it you will need the two patterned counters that we gave you at the start of your mission. The message consists of five bands of symbols, each divided into two rows. First translate the symbols into letters. Use the counter with the symbol ☙ to translate the symbols in the top row, and the counter with the symbol ☆ for the bottom row. Once all the symbols are translated, read along each band to uncover the message.
R.P.

What do the symbols say?

27

The Jumbled Symbols of Guana

OFFICIAL SURVEY OF ANCIENT BILONGI LANGUAGES –
VOLUME 6, APPENDIX 4

GUANA ISLAND - ANCIENT SYMBOLS

A
AND
BANYANA
BUILT
DANCE
DRAGON
FEAST
FIREBIRD
GREAT
HAPU
HIS
HAS
HEARD
INKURA
IS
JOKALA
JUNGLE
KILUMENA
KINJA

LANKALI
LIKALA
LOWER
MAGICIAN
MANIKI
MESSENGER
MOUNTAIN
NO
ON
OYSTER
POET
RIVER
SNAKES
SONG
STRONGHOLD
THAN
THE
TREASURE
TREES
WHICH
WONDER

From the inscriptions on the snake painting, Sally Cameron knows that Hapu left the island of Tiki and set course for distant Guana Island. Is this where he set up his legendary stronghold? Sally returns to her boat and sails to Guana. Exploring the island's shores, she comes across a stone marked with an arrow. Further along the beach, she finds another, and soon she is following a winding trail.

The trail ends at a cave where Sally finds an ancient painting of the island. A row of pictograms runs below the painting. With the help of her notes, Sally translates the symbols into English, but the words are strangely jumbled. Could the patterns above the painting reveal how they have been rearranged?

What do the symbols say?

The Secret of the Chart

Following in the footsteps of Lo Chi, Carrie Jones sets out for the pagoda of Ho Min Xen, high on the plateau of Noh. When she reaches the pagoda, she finds that it is now in ruins, and there is no sign of Lo Chi's message. Carrie goes to the nearby village of Chang Xi, where she discovers that a hundred years ago a band of marauders looted the pagoda. Many of the stolen treasures were lost forever, but a few were recovered and are now kept at the village.

To my devoted followers,

You are nearing the end of your journey. The dial and papers that you will find with this letter conceal the name of the remote mountain village where I have left my final set of instructions.

- Look at the first column of symbols on the piece of paper below. The top symbol is a full circle, and underneath is the symbol ▭. Find the full circle on the chart, then the symbol ▭ around its rim. Draw an imaginary line from the middle of the circle, through the symbol ▭ and across the chart.

- Return to the paper below. Repeat the process for the two symbols at the bottom of the first column.

- You now have two imaginary lines crossing the chart. Where the two lines meet you will find a symbol.

- Set the dial so that ▭ = H, and find the letter that corresponds to the symbol you have found on the chart.

- Continue until the message is revealed.

May you grow in wisdom and happiness,
Lo Chi

Sorting through the recovered treasures, Carrie finds a collection of papers and objects hidden in the folds of a silk painting. Excitedly, she spots a letter signed by Lo Chi, together with a dial, a small scroll and a complex chart. The letter tells her that these curious objects conceal a secret message revealing the name of the village where Lo Chi left his final instructions.

What is the name of the village?

The Dingbat File

From the message in the secret radio room, Mat Smith knows that Dingbat agents sent details of the location of the Red Panther headquarters to a special bunker in the city of Satroika. Mat takes the midnight plane to Satroika. With the help of contacts in the secret service, he discovers that the bunker is still in use. He finds his way there and explains his mission to the Head of Operations who leads him through a maze of corridors to the Central Control Room.

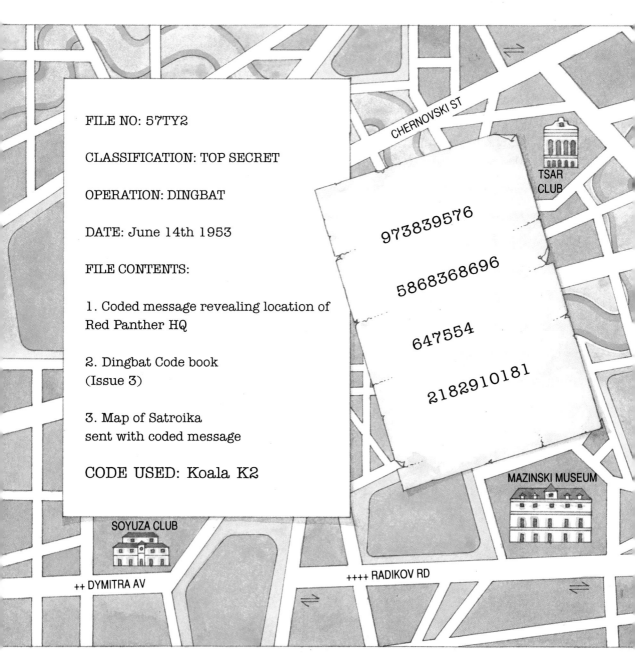

FILE NO: 57TY2

CLASSIFICATION: TOP SECRET

OPERATION: DINGBAT

DATE: June 14th 1953

FILE CONTENTS:

1. Coded message revealing location of Red Panther HQ

2. Dingbat Code book (Issue 3)

3. Map of Satroika sent with coded message

CODE USED: Koala K2

973839576

5868368696

647554

2182910181

CHERNOVSKI ST

TSAR CLUB

MAZINSKI MUSEUM

SOYUZA CLUB

++ DYMITRA AV

++++ RADIKOV RD

Here, he is handed a file marked DINGBAT:TOP SECRET. The file contains a typed card, a code book, a street map and a piece of paper with rows of numbers on it. The numbers form a coded message. With the help of instructions in the code book, Mat can decipher the message and at last locate the secret headquarters of the Red Panther Ring.

Where are the headquarters?

OPERATION DINGBAT:
CODE BOOK ISSUE 3

Code 15: KOALA K2

Brief description:
Koala K2 is a grid based code involving keywords.

Encoding instructions:
1. The basic grid for Koala K2 looks like this:

```
    1 2 3 4 5 6 7
  8 □ □ □ □ □ □ □
  9 □ □ □ □ □ □ □
  0 □ □ □ □ □ □ □
    □ □ □ □ □
```

Choose a series of keywords. Each keyword must contain seven different letters, and can be taken from any document. Enclose the document with the coded message and mark the first keyword with the symbol +, the second with the symbols ++, the third with the symbol +++ and so on.

Write the first keyword along the top row of the grid. Then write out the remaining letters of the alphabet in the spaces below. This is how the grid would look if the keyword was LEOPARD:

```
    1 2 3 4 5 6 7
    L E O P A R D
  8 B C F G H I J
  9 K M N Q S T U
  0 V W X Y Z
```

2. Translate the letters of the message into numbers. Letters in the top row of the grid are replaced by the number above them. In the LEOPARD grid, L=1, E=2 etc. Letters in the other rows are replaced by two numbers: the number at the beginning of the row, followed by the number at the top of the column. In the LEOPARD grid B=81, C=82 etc.

3. Change the keyword every six letters. You will need to draw a new grid for each new keyword.

Sam Hayley's Cipher

May 30th – Sam Hayley's message arrived this morning. As arranged, he wrote it in code. Using his grid, I have deciphered the information and now I am ready to plan the attack.

May 31st – Gough and the others escaped with $7000 of gold from the Maryville robbery, but Hank Knott was captured. We have buried the gold in a remote spot in Gable Canyon, and now we will ride across the Red Mountains into the next county where we can lie low for the next few months. I have written down the name of the place where the gold is hidden using Hayley's code. The keyword is Hayley's nickname.

```
B   B   C   E
H   X   U   D
E   S   J   E
F   C   C   A
```

The new railroad from Maryville to Fort Bloomsburg was opened by Governor James Chichester III amid great celebrations on Tuesday afternoon. The Governor praised all those whose courage and determination had made "the railroad dream" come true. However, there was controversy in the air when railroad owner Sam "Turncoat" Hayley rose to make his inaugural speech. Many remember the trial five years ago when Hayley was accused of abetting the notorious outlaw, ... Although cleared, there is ... ...dence that Hayley was guilty ...

...her unease. ...s of arrests ...linger Tom ...showdown ...on Saloon ...the crime ...ed out of ...at sunset ...bouts are ...ions are ...sehoods ...utation ... in the

MELROSE'S PATENT GUNPOWDER

Hayley's message. Keyword: Mustang

```
M   U   S   T   A   N   G   M   U   S   T
B   Y   X   D   Y   F   F   S   S   X   P
↓   ↓   ↓   ↓   ↓   ↓   ↓   ↓   ↓   ↓   ↓
C   O   N   S   I   G   N   M   E   N   T

A   N   G   M   U   S   T   A   N   G   M
B   Z   P   W   X   M   R   Y   S   K   I
↓   ↓   ↓   ↓   ↓   ↓   ↓   ↓   ↓   ↓   ↓
O   F   G   O   L   D   W   I   L   L   B

U   S   T   A   N   G   M   U   S   T   A
S   E   E   P   I   B   G   I   J   F   Y
↓   ↓   ↓   ↓   ↓   ↓   ↓   ↓   ↓   ↓   ↓
E   O   N   M   A   I   L   T   R   A   I

N   G   M   U   S   T   A   N   G   G
W   N   W   E   E   V   K   T   C
↓   ↓   ↓   ↓   ↓   ↓   ↓   ↓   ↓
N   T   O   M   O   R   R   O   W
```

Kate Jonson sets out in search of Ben Pierce's secret hideaway, deep in the wild Red Mountains. After three days struggling along steep mountain trails, she reaches her goal, a cave in Kutter's Canyon. Kate begins to search the cave, which is littered with packing cases, sticks of dynamite and broken bottles. In one corner, she spots an old bundle of sacks. Among them, she finds a collection of yellowed papers.

	A	B	C	D	E	F	G	H	I	J	K	L	M	N	O	P	Q	R	S	T	U	V	W	X	Y	Z
A	W	T	C	A	U	X	E	L	Y	J	V	D	P	I	B	R	O	K	Z	F	Q	M	H	G	S	N
B	T	C	A	U	X	E	L	Y	J	V	D	P	I	B	R	O	K	Z	F	Q	M	H	G	S	N	W
C	C	A	U	X	E	L	Y	J	V	D	P	I	B	R	O	K	Z	F	Q	M	H	G	S	N	W	T
D	A	U	X	E	L	Y	J	V	D	P	I	B	R	O	K	Z	F	Q	M	H	G	S	N	W	T	C
E	U	X	E	L	Y	J	V	D	P	I	B	R	O	K	Z	F	Q	M	H	G	S	N	W	T	C	A
F	X	E	L	Y	J	V	D	P	I	B	R	O	K	Z	F	Q	M	H	G	S	N	W	T	C	A	U
G	E	L	Y	J	V	D	P	I	B	R	O	K	Z	F	Q	M	H	G	S	N	W	T	C	A	U	X
H	L	Y	J	V	D	P	I	B	R	O	K	Z	F	Q	M	H	G	S	N	W	T	C	A	U	X	E
I	Y	J	V	D	P	I	B	R	O	K	Z	F	Q	M	H	G	S	N	W	T	C	A	U	X	E	L
J	J	V	D	P	I	B	R	O	K	Z	F	Q	M	H	G	S	N	W	T	C	A	U	X	E	L	Y
K	V	D	P	I	B	R	O	K	Z	F	Q	M	H	G	S	N	W	T	C	A	U	X	E	L	Y	J
L	D	P	I	B	R	O	K	Z	F	Q	M	H	G	S	N	W	T	C	A	U	X	E	L	Y	J	V
M	P	I	B	R	O	K	Z	F	Q	M	H	G	S	N	W	T	C	A	U	X	E	L	Y	J	V	D
N	I	B	R	O	K	Z	F	Q	M	H	G	S	N	W	T	C	A	U	X	E	L	Y	J	V	D	P
O	B	R	O	K	Z	F	Q	M	H	G	S	N	W	T	C	A	U	X	E	L	Y	J	V	D	P	I
P	R	O	K	Z	F	Q	M	H	G	S	N	W	T	C	A	U	X	E	L	Y	J	V	D	P	I	B
Q	O	K	Z	F	Q	M	H	G	S	N	W	T	C	A	U	X	E	L	Y	J	V	D	P	I	B	R
R	K	Z	F	Q	M	H	G	S	N	W	T	C	A	U	X	E	L	Y	J	V	D	P	I	B	R	O
S	Z	F	Q	M	H	G	S	N	W	T	C	A	U	X	E	L	Y	J	V	D	P	I	B	R	O	K
T	F	Q	M	H	G	S	N	W	T	C	A	U	X	E	L	Y	J	V	D	P	I	B	R	O	K	Z
U	Q	M	H	G	S	N	W	T	C	A	U	X	E	L	Y	J	V	D	P	I	B	R	O	K	Z	F
V	M	H	G	S	N	W	T	C	A	U	X	E	L	Y	J	V	D	P	I	B	R	O	K	Z	F	Q
W	H	G	S	N	W	T	C	A	U	X	E	L	Y	J	V	D	P	I	B	R	O	K	Z	F	Q	M
X	G	S	N	W	T	C	A	U	X	E	L	Y	J	V	D	P	I	B	R	O	K	Z	F	Q	M	H
Y	S	N	W	T	C	A	U	X	E	L	Y	J	V	D	P	I	B	R	O	K	Z	F	Q	M	H	G
Z	N	W	T	C	A	U	X	E	L	Y	J	V	D	P	I	B	R	O	K	Z	F	Q	M	H	G	S

One of these is a page ripped from a diary. According to this, the scribbled letters on one of the scraps of paper form a coded message revealing where the gang hid the gold stolen from the Maryville mail train. If Kate can decipher the message, she will be able to name the hiding place and so fulfil her quest.

Where is the gold hidden?

Clocktower Communication

THIS PAINTING SHOWS THE GRAND PARADE AT THE MASQUE
4   5   6   3   3   2   1
10   7   11 11 8 8 7

JONES. THE MASQUE WAS HELD TO CELEBRATE THE
3   4   4   6   6
12   9   11   7   9

THE GRAND PARADE WAS LED BY THE KING HIMSELF. HE WAS
1   5   2   5   3   2   3   6
12 9   11 11   9   9 10   10

MARIANNE, MONSIEUR JEAN DE LA TOUBIERE, MADAME

To Roland Petanque,

I have discovered that Le Capitaine is planning to thwart the Montero Society's plot to steal the Sargasso Jewels. I have intercepted a message sent between two of Le Capitaine's allies, and this reveals his true identity. To decipher the message, you must take the 36 marked letters from the painting and write them on the fan. To do this, look at the two numbers beneath the first marked letter. Translate these numbers into musical notes, using the lanterns as a key. The two musical notes will enable you to pinpoint a single position on the fan. Write the first marked letter in this position, then continue in the same way until you have written all the marked letters onto the fan. Finally, read the message, which winds around the fan in a strange but predictable way.

Monsieur Thomas

Ben Harvey sets off for the town of Latoures. Four hundred years ago, Monsieur Thomas was ordered to leave communications to the Montero Society above the doorway of the clocktower in the town square. Could any messages still be there centuries later?

To his amazement, Ben finds a loose stone above the door, and pulls it away to reveal a small niche. Inside, he finds a tightly wrapped bundle. It contains a letter, a small painting and a fan. If Ben can decipher a message hidden in the painting and fan, he will finally discover the true identity of Le Capitaine.

OF LANTERNS, DEVISED BY THE INGENIOUS POET, ORLANDO

5	1	6	1	1	6	2
12	8	12	9	11	8	10

BIRTHDAY OF OUR ILLUSTRIOUS SOVEREIGN, HENRI XVIII.

1	4	5	5
10	12	10	8

FOLLOWED BY THE MARQUIS OF ST PIERRE, THE DUCHESS OF

4	4	3	2	2
8	7	7	12	7

ANNETTE DE GOUACHE AND MONSIEUR PAUL DELAMARE

What is Le Capitaine's real name?

37

Pavilion Puzzle

To my devoted followers,
I have taken refuge in the Pavilion of
So Shong which lies just outside the
village of Tian Song. You must find your
way to the smallest room in the pavilion.
This is my secret chamber. Be warned:
two rooms in the building have been
boobytrapped by my faithful servant, Lo
Pin. With this letter, you will find a
coded plan of the pavilion. Use this to
find the safe route to my chamber. The
following explanations will help you make
sense of the plan.

Scale

1 2 3 4

Lines

Room

)(Door

Rooms connected by door

Stairs connecting two rooms on
different floors

Booby trap. DO NOT ENTER

I trust that we shall meet again very
soon.
May you grow in wisdom and happiness,
Lo Chi

After a perilous journey across the
Chi Nen Mountains, Carrie Jones
reaches the village of Tian Song
where she retrieves Lo Chi's final set
of instructions. These consist of an
elaborate scroll, a picture of the
nearby Pavilion of So Shong and a
parchment covered with symbols.

According to the scroll, Lo Chi took
refuge in the pavilion, and his secret
chamber was the smallest room. The
symbols on the parchment form a
coded plan of the building. If Carrie
can make sense of the symbols, she
will be able to locate Lo Chi's
chamber. Then she will be able to
find a safe route to it and finally
retrieve the vital message left by
Thomas Hudson.

What is her route?

Pavilion of So Shong

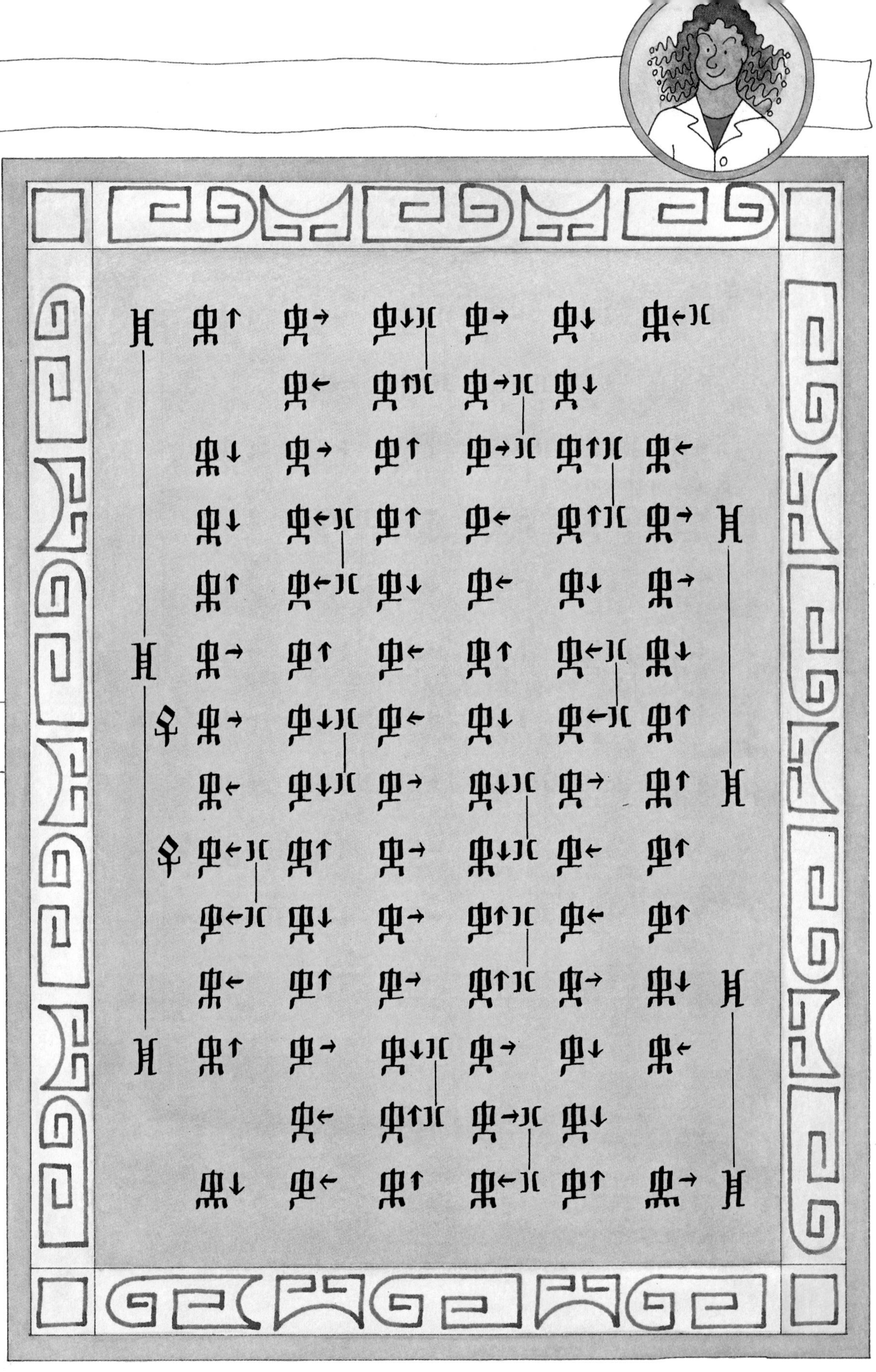

Thomas Hudson's Final Challenge

Carrie Jones rushes up the steps of the Rialto Hotel clutching the vital message that she retrieved from Lo Chi's secret chamber. She races to room 501 where Mat Smith, Kate Jonson, Sally Cameron and Ben Harvey have already assembled in time for Thomas Hudson's six o'clock deadline. As a clock strikes the hour, a mysterious figure in dark glasses walks slowly into the room. He places a sealed envelope on the table, then leaves.

To Mat Smith, Kate Jonson, Ben Harvey, Sally Cameron and Carrie Jones

Welcome back from your adventures! If you have all successfully completed your missions, you will now be ready to take on my final challenge. Using the two grids and the dial that you will find with this letter, you must decode the message which was left in Lo Chi's secret refuge. This reveals the location of the lost treasures of the ancient Bilongi civilization.

I encoded the name of the hiding place using a cipher which I devised myself:

First I wrote the name of the headquarters of the Red Panther Spy Ring across the top of the small grid, followed by the remaining letters of the alphabet. Using the grid, I then converted each letter of the treasures' location into two symbols by writing down the symbol at the beginning of the row, followed by the symbol at the top of the column.

Next I erased the letters from the grid, and across the top, I wrote the name of the mountain where Hapu built his stronghold, followed by the remaining letters of the alphabet. Then I used the grid to convert the real name of Le Capitaine into symbols.

I took the first symbol of the treasures' location and the first symbol of Le Capitaine's name and converted them into a number, using the large grid. I repeated this process until all the symbols were translated into numbers.

With the help of the dial, I converted the numbers into letters. For the first two numbers, I set the dial so that 1 represented the first letter of the name of the place where Pierce and his gang hid the loot from the Maryville mail train. For the second two numbers I set the dial so that 1 represented the second letter, and so on, until I reached the end.

If you can decode the message, you will be able to find the long lost treasures and embark on an exciting life of adventure. If you fail, then only obscurity beckons ...

Good luck,

Thomas Hudson.

Ripping open the envelope, the adventurers find a letter from Thomas Hudson. This tells them that the information they have uncovered holds the key to the vital message that Carrie retrieved. If they can decode the message, they will discover the location of the lost treasures of the Bilongi civilization. If not, the secret will remain hidden for ever.

Where are the lost treasures?

	Ω	Π	Δ	Σ	Φ	∂	ℵ	ℑ	℘	ε	ψ	α
Ω	4	23	5	7	6	14	21	18	9	3	6	12
Π	23	7	18	1	20	10	22	3	23	13	8	4
Δ	5	18	3	8	17	15	9	23	5	4	6	14
Σ	7	1	8	24	6	14	21	2	9	3	23	5
Φ	6	20	17	6	8	24	18	1	20	10	25	2
∂	14	10	15	14	24	19	18	9	3	5	12	17
ℵ	21	22	9	21	18	18	3	6	14	21	17	8
ℑ	18	3	23	2	1	9	6	7	25	8	23	13
℘	9	23	5	9	20	3	14	25	9	14	21	19
ε	3	13	4	3	10	5	21	8	14	11	7	6
ψ	6	8	6	23	25	12	17	23	21	7	2	18
α	12	4	14	5	2	17	8	13	19	6	18	9

B D A C Q N D B
A K B F J U Y U
E A V V C Z K W
X A Y W H T P S

AKOA CAVE   ANI BAY

IKOALI FOREST

SATUMA RIVER

METENA POINT

Clues

Pages 4-5

To find out which code has been used for the first message, work through the instructions for each code in reverse. By a process of trial and error, you will find out which code has been used. Decode the other messages in the same way.

Pages 6-7

The scrap of paper is the key to crack this message. Then just follow Pierce's instructions exactly. A message should soon start to appear.

Pages 8-9

Read Henri de la Motte's letter carefully. It does not matter which side of the playing cards you use!

Pages 10-11

As the word U is the only single letter word in the ancient Bilongi language, the letter U must correspond to the symbol ≋ on the parchment. Now look at the last word in the third line. The last letter of this word is U. How many six-letter words ending with U can you find in the list? You should now know which symbols correspond to T, E, O and N. From here, it should be quite easy to identify which symbols relate to the other English letters.

Pages 12-13

Treat this boardgame as a jigsaw puzzle. Start with the two cross shaped pieces. And remember – each piece can only be used once!

Pages 14-15

Start by trying to discover how each scrambler switch rearranges the symbols. Now assume that the first switch has been used to encode the message. What order would the symbols have been in originally? Try translating the reordered symbols into letters. Does a message start to appear? If not, try the other two scrambling orders.

Pages 16-17

Once you have discovered how the coding device works, it should be quite easy to rearrange the lines in the diary. Imagine sliding the symbol on the 'Coded Line' part of the ruler so that it is above the same symbol on the 'Original Line' section of the ruler.

Pages 18-19

Start by writing out the message without the numbers or symbols. You should then be able to fill in some of the spaces with the missing letters and consequently discover which three numbers or symbols have been used for each letter.

Pages 20-21

Start with the following two sentences:
'Adiki struck Oba'
'Adiki sailed away'.
The word 'Adiki' appears in both of these sentences. As the only symbol the sentences have in common is 朼, this must mean Adiki.

Pages 22-23

Follow the letter closely. Lo Chi's instructions are very clear, but it is a long process.

Pages 24-25

Work through the encoding instructions in reverse to uncover the original message. You will need to use all the papers on these pages.

Page 26

The size of the letters is the key to this puzzle. But you will need to fill in the large disk as well.

Page 27

Could the shapes on the picture have any connection with the shapes surrounding the letters on the counters?

Page 28-29

Translating the symbols is the easy part. Remember that the pattern above the painting shows how the pictograms have been encoded, so you will have to work from right to left to decode them.

Pages 30-31

Lo Chi has yet again written very clear instructions! Follow them exactly to reveal the message. Don't forget to reset the wheel as instructed.

Pages 32-33

Remember to draw a new grid for each keyword. Then just translate the numbers back into letters.

Pages 34-35

Knowing the keyword is crucial for deciphering this message. You will find it in the news clipping. Now look at Hayley's message. The coded letters are typewritten. Can you make sense of the letters that Pierce has added? The large grid will help.

Pages 36-37

Follow Monsieur Thomas's letter exactly. Once you have written all the letters on the fan, read off the message starting in the bottom right-hand corner.

Pages 38-39

Look carefully at the explanation on Lo Chi's scroll. It may be simpler than it seems. Squared paper will help you to draw the plan. You should be able to plot a route to the smallest room – and remember to look out for the booby traps.

Pages 40-41

Work through Thomas Hudson's encoding process in reverse to reveal where the treasures are hidden. You will only be able to solve this code if you already know the answers to the puzzles on pages 28-29, 32-33, 34-35 and 36-37. Remember to draw the grids exactly as instructed, and follow the code step by step. This puzzle is not easy!

Answers

Pages 4-5

By a process of trial and error, Mat discovers which code has been used for each telegram. Then he can figure out what they say. Here are the translated messages with punctuation added:

ALMARO EXPRESS: TO SEAGULL FROM EAGLE. YOU ARE INSTRUCTED TO TAKE COMMAND OF OPERATION DINGBAT.
(Code TL4: Oranges and Lemons)

ADESSA TELEGRAMS: TO ALBATROSS FROM FALCON. REPORT TO SEAGULL AT THE MINISTRY OF COUNTER ESPIONAGE IN BALAIKA CITY.
(Code TL1: Mustard and Cress)

QST: TO SEAGULL FROM MACAW. RED PANTHER AGENTS HAVE INFILTRATED THE ALBONI RESEARCH INSTITUTE.
(Code TL3: Lobster Pot)

SENDERO TELEGRAMS: TO EAGLE AND RAVEN FROM SEAGULL. CARRY OUT SURVEILLANCE OPERATION AT ALBONI RESEARCH INSTITUTE. IDENTIFY RED PANTHER INFILTRATORS.
(Code TL5: Deadly Nightshade)

HALVANIA TELEGRAMS: TO SEAGULL FROM FALCON. WE HAVE IDENTIFIED AND ARRESTED ALBONI INFILTRATORS BUT RED PANTHER IS PLANNING NEW OPERATION AT UNKNOWN LOCATION – POSSIBLY OTHER RESEARCH ESTABLISHMENT.
(Code TL6: Laughing Demons)

Pages 6-7

Following Pierce's instructions, Kate pieces together the following message:

> JOE GOUGH WILL HOLD UP THE MARYVILLE MAIL TRAIN ON MAY 31ST. YOU WILL TRAVEL AS PASSENGERS ON THE TRAIN. WHEN IT REACHES THE KLONDIKE PASS, FORCE THE DRIVER TO STOP.

Pages 8-9

Ben works through Henri de la Motte's letter. He finds two symbols from the playing cards, then uses these as a reference for the diamond-shaped grid.

He discovers that the meeting was to take place at CHATEAU LOT.

Pages 10-11

Once she knows which symbol corresponds with each letter, Sally can easily translate the inscriptions. This is what they say:

ON MIDSUMMER DAY, THE GREAT HERO, HAPU, WAS BORN ON THE ISLAND OF TIKI. HIS MOTHER WAS KAIA, WHO KNEW THE MEANING OF DREAMS, AND HIS FATHER WAS OBA THE FISHERMAN.

Pages 12-13

With all the pieces in place, the board looks like this:

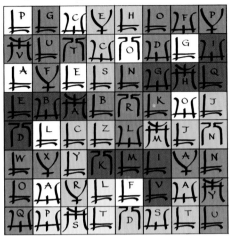

Reading the exposed letters in order, Carrie discovers that the next set of instructions was left at the PALACE OF GO.

Pages 14-15

Mat soon realizes that the symbols have been encoded using the third scrambling order. The other scrambling orders do not produce a message.

Working through the instructions on the blueprint in reverse, he uncovers the following message:

RADIO ROOM IS IN SCHOTT TOWER IN KAMAROV FOREST.

Pages 16-17

Using the coding device, Kate puts the lines of the diary entry into their original order. Then she reinstates the correct punctuation. This is what the diary says:

May 31st '84

I set off with Hank Knott at sunrise and we took up our positions in the Klondike Pass, waiting for the train to appear. At noon exactly, we heard the sound of a distant engine.

"Prepare to strike!" I yelled at Hank.

Minutes later the train came into view. We both knew the plan by heart. Danny Heape and Jake Sharp were aboard, and would force the driver to stop. At their signal, we'd attack.

The train screeched to a sudden halt. The plan was working! We rushed to the train, smashed open the doors of the mail van and grabbed the sacks of gold.

But at that moment I saw a column of horsemen riding in our direction. They were led by our old enemy, Marshal Jack Davenport! We raced back to our horses, staggering under the weight of the gold. Suddenly I saw Hank Knott stumble. Davenport rode straight at him. Hank scrambled to his feet, but seconds later he was in the marshal's clutches.

The rest of us leaped back onto our horses and galloped away from the scene. But Davenport was hot on our heels. We tore along the mountain trails, driving our horses as hard as we could, and at last we managed to outride our pursuers. We laid low until nightfall, then set out for the secret hideaway. But when we arrived, Pierce was waiting for us with bad news. Hank Knott had been taken to Fort Davenport and had betrayed us! He had even handed over details of the location of our hideaway. We buried the loot in a secret place, then fled into the next county.

Pages 18-19

Once Ben has discovered which numbers and symbols have been used for each letter, he can easily decode the message. The key is shown here:

A = 6, 4,   O = 1, 3, *
E = ¿, 2, 9   U = ¶, §, 7
I = ¡, 5, 8

This is what the writing says:

As soon as the meeting opened, the Duke of Thierry announced that Le Capitaine had thwarted our activities for a third time. Five members of the Society were caught red handed during the attempt to steal the Orlando Diamonds and they are now rotting in the Carcelle prison. The Duke demanded that we discover the identity of Le Capitaine so that we can eliminate him once and for all. Immediately, Roland Petanque leaped to his feet announcing that he had hired a certain Monsieur Thomas to discover his true identity. Monsieur Thomas is one of the most cunning rogues in the whole kingdom. The Duke was pleased at the news and offered to reward Monsieur Thomas with five hundred francs if he succeeds.

Pages 20-21

By a process of deduction, Sally figures out the meaning of each of the ancient symbols. Then she translates the symbols on the snake into English.

Finally she puts the words into the right order, using the sentences on Anita Raia's notes as a model. This is what the inscriptions say:

THE EARTHQUAKE STRUCK TIKI.
THE ISLANDERS LEFT TIKI.
HAPU LED ONE GROUP.
KINJA LED ANOTHER GROUP.
HAPU SAILED TO GUANA.

Pages 22-23

Following Lo Chi's instructions, Carrie uncovers the following message:

GO TO THE PAGODA OF HO MIN XEN AND FIND THE KEEPER OF THE ROBES.

Pages 24-25

Working backward through the directions in the code book, Mat reveals the following message:

RED PANTHER HQ LOCATED. DETAILS SENT TO BUNKER IN SATROIKA.

Page 26

First, Kate fills in the missing numbers on the large disk. The completed disk is shown on the right.

Next she follows Pierce's directions to discover that the hideaway is in STOKER'S CAVERN. This is marked near the top of the map.

Page 27

Using the shapes on the disks as a key, Ben uncovers the following message:
CLOCKTOWER IN LATOURES, ABOVE THE DOORWAY.

Pages 28-29

Using the lists of symbols, Sally translates the pictograms into English. Then, examining the patterns at the top of the painting, she realizes that they have been rearranged in the following stages:

1. The symbols are written out in a spiral:

2. The vertical columns are reordered:

3. The symbols are read off in a zigzag:

4 5 1 3 2

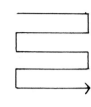

Sally works through this process in reverse to reveal the following message:

> THE GREAT HAPU BUILT HIS STRONGHOLD ON KILUMENA MOUNTAIN, WHICH IS LOWER THAN LANKALI MOUNTAIN. INKURA MOUNTAIN HAS NO SNAKES. MANIKI MOUNTAIN HAS NO RIVER.

Pages 30-31

Using the yellow piece of paper, Carrie finds the following symbols on the large chart:

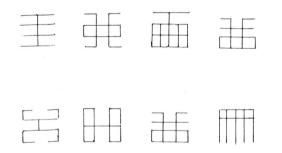

She then uses the code wheel to translate them into letters. She discovers that Lo Chi's refuge was in the village of TIAN SONG.

Pages 32-33

First of all, Mat finds the four keywords, which are all road names on the map. They are:

1. SMETYNA
2. DYMITRA
3. YVESTIA
4. RADIKOV

Now he can draw the grids and decipher the numbers to reveal the following message:

RED PANTHER HQ IS AT TSAR CLUB.

Pages 34-35

From the news clipping, Kate learns that Hayley's nickname was 'Turncoat'.

Using this as the keyword, she decodes Pierce's message. She discovers that the gold was hidden at the VULTURES' NEST ROCK.

Pages 36-37

First, Ben writes the marked letters onto the fan. Then he reads off the message starting in the bottom right-hand corner. The completed fan is shown here.

The message reads:

TRUST JEAN DE LA TOUBIERE.
HE IS LE CAPITAINE.

Pages 38-39

Following the instructions in Lo Chi's letter, Carrie draws the plan of the Pagoda shown here.

She knows that Lo Chi's chamber was the smallest room in the building. This is marked with a cross. To reach it, Carrie must go through the numbered rooms in order. Rooms connected by stairs are joined with a curved line.

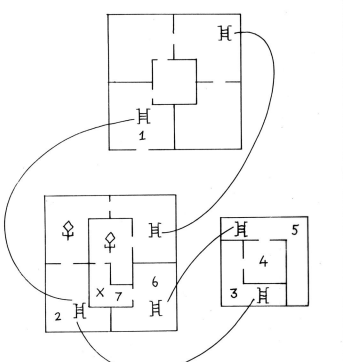

Pages 40-41

Working through Thomas Hudson's instructions in reverse, the five adventurers discover that the Bilongi treasures are hidden in ANI CAVE IN AKOA BAY. This is shown on the right of the map.

First published in 1994 by Usborne Publishing Ltd, Usborne House, 83-85 Saffron Hill, London EC1N 8RT, England.

Copyright © 1994 Usborne Publishing Ltd.

The name Usborne and the device 🎈 are Trade Marks of Usborne Publishing Ltd.

Printed in Spain   U.E.
First published in America March 1995